GRACIE
SAVES THE DAY!

Written by:
Catherine Gibson
&
Michael LaChance

Illustrated by:
Rebekah Phillips

For Children With
Love Publications LLC
Farmington, CT

For Children With Love Publications, LLC
P.O. Box 1552
Farmington, Connecticut 06034
www.forchildrenwithlove.com

ISBN 978-0-9831221-8-0 hard cover
ISBN 978-0-9831221-9-7 soft cover

Publisher's Cataloging-In-Publication Data
(Prepared by The Donohue Group, Inc.)

Names: Gibson, Catherine (Catherine Czerwinski). | LaChance, Michael, 1966- | Phillips, Rebekah, 1982- illustrator.
Title: Gracie saves the day! / written by: Catherine Gibson & Michael LaChance ; illustrations: Rebekah Phillips.
Description: Farmington, Connecticut : For Children With Love Publications, [2017] | Interest age level: 005-008. | Summary: "Gracie loves baseball. The meanest girl in school, Penelope Taylor always makes fun of her for liking 'boys' stuff.' When Gracie's friend Mary wants them to enter a school dance contest together, Penelope's teasing gets even worse. Out of jealousy, she tries to ruin Mary's chances at winning, but Gracie saves the day, just by being herself."-- Provided by publisher.
Identifiers: ISBN 978-0-9831221-8-0 (hard cover) | ISBN 978-0-9831221-9-7 (soft cover)
Subjects: LCSH: Bullying--Juvenile fiction. | Friendship--Juvenile fiction. | Dance--Competitions--Juvenile fiction. | Helping behavior--Juvenile fiction. | CYAC: Bullying--Fiction. | Friendship--Fiction. | Dance--Competitions--Juvenile fiction. | Helpfulness--Fiction.
Classification: LCC PZ7.G339264 Gr 2017 (hard cover) | LCC PZ7.G339264 (soft cover) | DDC [E]--dc23

Printed in the U.S.A

Dedicated to Alyssa and Kylee Czerwinski.

The kindest & coolest girls I know!

Penelope Taylor was the meanest, crankiest girl in the whole school. She thought she was perfect. She wore perfect dresses, her nails were perfectly done, and she always wore a perfect bow in her hair.

"Poor Gracie, wearing that dirty baseball shirt again?" Penelope snickered. "When are you going to dress and act like a girl?"

Gracie and her best friend Joey kept walking out of school toward the bus.

Joey shook his head, "I know you get along with just about everybody, but you have to admit, Gracie, it's even hard for you to get along with Penelope Taylor," he muttered.

Gracie gave him a little smile. "Besides," Joey continued, "You love sports. And you're good at them. You can hit, kick, and throw things better than most of us guys."

Gracie's smile stretched into a grin, "And most of all, I love baseball!" she said.

"Yeah, and you're so good, us guys picked you first for our team!" Joey and Gracie slapped a high five just as they heard their friend Mary call from the school steps.

1

Mary ran toward them waving a piece of paper. "You guys! Check this out!" she shouted. Several of their friends heard her and gathered around. Mary handed the paper to Gracie. "Please do this with me. I can't do it without you."

But before Gracie could read what it said, Penelope snatched it out of her hand. "A dance contest? Oh, how wonderful!" She twirled around the crowd holding the paper in the air.

"Let me see it," Gracie said.

Penelope threw it at her. "Don't bother. This is for girls only."

"Hey! Gracie is a girl." said Mary.

"Oh, she is?" Penelope looked Gracie up and down. "Then why does she always dress and act like a boy?"

Just then, Principal Goldsmith walked toward them, and everyone scattered except Gracie. Gracie just stood there.

"Are you okay, Gracie?" Principal Goldsmith asked.

"I'm fine," hiding her tears.

When Gracie arrived home, she stormed into her house, dropped her backpack on the kitchen floor, slid down the wall, and just sat there.

Her mom joined Gracie on the floor. "How was your day?"

"Mary really wants me to enter the school dance contest with her, but I'm not a dancer," she said. "And besides, I don't have anything to wear."

"Why don't you do it just for fun?" Mom asked, and reached for her hand to help her off the floor. "Come on, I have an idea that might help you make up your mind."

Gracie had never been in a store like the Ballet Boutique. She felt uncomfortable, even when Miss Lulu smiled at them from behind the counter.

"How may I help you?" she asked.

"We're looking for an outfit for a school dance contest," Mom replied.

Miss Lulu showed them every dress in the store, but nothing seemed right. Then Gracie peeked into a white box on the counter shaped like a tutu. She opened it and saw the most beautiful tutu she had ever seen. Her eyes lit up. "Maybe dressing up won't be so bad. This tutu is a winner!"

But Miss Lulu pointed to a yellow tag hanging from it. "Oh, goodness. I'm sorry," she said, "but this tutu is reserved for someone else. I'm actually expecting her in now."

Gracie's heart sank. The bell above the door chimed and Miss Lulu took the tutu from the hanger. Gracie didn't want to see the lucky girl who owned the tutu. She tugged on Mom's sleeve. "Let's go," she whispered.

"Do you like my dress?" a familiar voice asked.

Gracie could only watch while Penelope held the tutu under her chin and swayed this way and that, and gazed at her perfect reflection in the mirror with the light bouncing off the sparkly dress.

Of course, it was the perfect dress for Penelope.

"With this, I'm sure to win first prize." Penelope said. She spun in a pretty pirouette.

Driving home, Mom said, "It's not what a dancer wears, but how she feels inside that makes her a great dancer."

Gracie frowned. "I don't care about all this stuff," she grumbled.

"Really? Then why are you entering the contest?" Mom asked.

"Because of that girl Penelope! She's always telling me how I look and act like a boy. Plus, Mary really wants me to dance with her."

"Gracie, don't change who you are for Penelope or anyone else," Mom said. "How about dancing for fun, instead?"

8

That night in bed, Gracie thought about what her mom had said.
She decided costume or no costume, she was going to be herself and
try her best, and have fun.

The next day, Gracie put on her cap, jersey, and shorts, and headed to baseball practice. Joey was on the pitcher's mound winding up.

"Grab a bat Gracie. I'll pitch you some balls."

Strike, Strike, Strike.

"Wow! You never strike out! What's wrong with you, Gracie?" asked Joey.

Gracie dropped her bat and tossed her hat to the ground.

"Penelope Taylor! That's what. She's always teasing me about what I wear and what I do!"

Joey jogged in from the pitcher's mound. When he got close, he said, "So what? You're a team player and Penelope's not. You're a friend no matter what people look like or what they wear. We like you just the way you are."

Gracie smiled slowly, then turned and sprinted away. Over her shoulder, she called back, "Thanks, Joey. You're the best! I gotta go. I have to practice a dance routine at Mary's."

11

Gracie rang the doorbell to apartment 12C. Mary answered the door.

"C'mon in," she said. "Mom, Gracie's here. We're going outside to practice."

"Wait a minute, said her mom. "I have something for you." She handed Mary a brown paper bag. Mary reached inside and pulled out a tutu. It wasn't brand new, but it still sparkled. She gave her mom a big hug and slipped it on.

"Do you like it, Gracie?" Mary asked.

"Yes! You look great!" Gracie said.

The girls went outside to practice. Mary helped Gracie create a simple but good routine, then practiced her own more complicated one. Gracie tried her best, but she kept tripping over her own feet. Mary stopped to help her every time. "Just keep practicing," she said. "You'll get it."

Soon a group of kids from the apartments circled around them and clapped while they danced.

Suddenly a voice spoke out from the crowd. "Mary, is that what you're wearing for the school dance contest?"

14

It was Penelope—again!

"You can't win wearing that old tutu," Penelope said. Then she turned to Gracie, "And you…! You should stick to baseball!"

Ignoring Penelope, Gracie put her arm around Mary. "Let's go. Who cares what she thinks."

Mary looked down at her costume. "But she's right," she whimpered. "I can't win in this. It's old."

Gracie took Mary's hands and looked her in the eyes. "You are the best dancer in the whole school. If you feel good and beautiful inside, you are the same outside. And I think your tutu is great!"

15

After weeks of practice, the dance contest was only one day away. Mary had perfected her dance routine, but Gracie still struggled with hers.

That night at dinner her dad asked, "Are you nervous, sweetie?"

Gracie shrugged her shoulders.

"Everyone gets nervous," said Mom.

"What are you going to wear," asked Dad.

Again, she shrugged her shoulders. Gracie watched her dad walk down the hall and open the closet door. Returning to the dinner table, holding a white box from Miss Lulu's Ballet Boutique. He placed the box in front of Gracie with a broad smile on his face.

Inside was a brand-new tutu that was even prettier than the one in the store—the one she'd fallen in love with that Penelope was going to wear. Jumping out of her chair, Gracie gave her parents big hugs.

"Thank you! Thank you!" she said.

Immediately, she tried it on, and it fit perfectly! She danced and twirled around, still stumbling over her feet, but Gracie was so happy she didn't care.

The next morning Gracie arrived at school in her cap, jersey, and shorts, and when it was time, she slipped into her new beautiful tutu and joined the other dancers backstage.

Penelope noticed Gracie's new costume right away. Her eyes narrowed. "Where did you get that?"

Gracie just smiled. "Do you like it?"

"No, I don't. But it won't matter anyway. You're clumsy and should stick to baseball," Penelope snickered.

Enough was enough! Gracie walked over to Penelope and stood nose to nose. "I love baseball. I don't care what you think!" said Gracie firmly.

Penelope stomped away from Gracie and pushed her way through the line of dancers waiting for the mirror. "It's my turn" she demanded, and elbowed Mary so hard she fell to the floor. There was a riiiiiiipping sound. All the other

Gracie ran to help her friend. When Mary dusted herself off, she saw the big tear down the side of her tutu and started to cry. She turned to Gracie. "I didn't care that my tutu wasn't the best, but I can't go out there with a big rip in it."

Gracie's mind raced. All around her stood girls in sparkly new tutus—and then there was Mary in her torn, wilted one. "Wait! I can fix this!" she said. She grabbed Mary's hand and pulled her into the dressing room.

The music began and the curtain opened. One by one each girl went out and danced her very best. The announcer then called for Gracie. Her song started to play. She ran out onto the stage dressed in her baseball cap, jersey and shorts and danced her routine just the way Mary had taught her.

Everyone was surprised and confused. Penelope laughed and pointed as she danced. Gracie didn't care. She was having fun!

The scores for all the dancers went up on a big board, and Penelope Taylor's name was at the very top. "I'm sure to win now!" she exclaimed.

Finally, Mary's dance routine began. When she danced into the spotlight, the other dancers were surprised to see her wearing Gracie's costume. She spun, twirled, and leapt like never before! She floated across the stage, and Gracie could not have been happier.

When Mary finished her dance, the crowd stood up and cheered! She ran over to Gracie and gave her a big hug.

Mary's mom and Gracie's parents were still standing and clapping.

From the audience, Joey chanted, "Mary! Mary! Mary!" and the other dancers joined in. Mary Myers name came up first on the board with a perfect ten right above Penelope Taylors's name. The crowd went wild!

Penelope ran off the stage, while all the girls surrounded Mary with a group hug. Gracie had never felt better about anything than she did at that moment.

Gracie caught Joey's eye, tipped her cap, and swung a pretend bat, as if she'd just hit a Grand Slam!

The End

Gracie Saves the Day!
Individual and group activities

1. Gracie loved sports. Sit in a group and share what outdoor games or sports you like to play? Can you play by yourself, or do you need a team to play?

2. Have you ever played a game or sport on a team? What happens when your team wins? How does it feel if your team loses? Can it be fun even if you don't win?

3. Have you ever been teased about playing sports or outdoor activities? How did you feel? Draw a picture or write about how you felt.

4. Have you ever been teased because you like to wear dresses, have your hair look 'just right'? How did you feel? Draw a picture or write a story about how you felt.

5. It hurt Gracie's feelings when Penelope made fun of her. Has anyone ever told you that you weren't acting like a girl? Or that you weren't acting boyish enough? What would you say to someone who teased you?

6. If you were Penelope's friend, what could you do to help her be a better friend to Gracie and others?

7. What can happen when you don't get along with someone in your school or a group you belong to? How do you feel? What can you do to get along better?

8. When a friend is upset, what can you do to help them feel better?

9. What are the two big things that Gracie did to help Mary? Are there other things she could have done? What would you have done?

10. Have you ever tried to do something new like Gracie did? What was it? What happened? Draw a picture or write about what happened.

11. Because Gracie had never danced before, she had to practice very hard to get ready for the dance contest. Have you ever had to practice hard for something? What was it? Write a story or draw a picture about that activity.

12. What is something new you would like to try that you haven't done before, or haven't done very often?

13. How did the story end? Were you surprised? If this were your story, how would you have ended the story?

About the Authors

Catherine Czerwinski Gibson is an award-winning author of six books for children, host of The Cathy Gibson TV Show and the founder of For Children With Love, an organization which supports various children's charities. The mother of two grown sons, Cathy fills her time creatively, writing children's books with a positive message and producing her TV show. At the heart of all of Cathy's work is finding ways to instill in children the joy inherent in showing kindness and respect to others. Cathy lives, writes and films her show in Connecticut.

Co-Author Michael LaChance is first and foremost a family man blessed with his wonderful wife Laura and two amazing boys, Tyler and Bryan. He is a creative story, script and songwriter as well as co-producer, director, puppeteer and voice impersonator for the Cathy Gibson Show. Michael loves to help kids by getting a message across through humor and levity. A native of Connecticut, Michael enjoys collaborating with his good friend Cathy Gibson.

www.forchildrenwithlove.com

About the Illustrator

Rebekah Phillips is a graduate of The Lyme Academy College of Fine Arts and has illustrated numerous children's picture books for other authors as well as three of her own, "Piper was Afraid," "Lily the Fancipoo" and "Mocha Grande." Orginally from Connecticut, she now resides in Sarasota Florida with her husband Kurt and her pug-mix puppy, Mocha. Rebekah hopes to inspire young minds with a love for the arts.

"Imagination is a beautiful gift...never stop dreaming!"

www.rebekahphillips.com

Catherine Gibson

Award Winning Author

Captivating, inspiring children's books teach acceptance and respect for ourselves and each other.

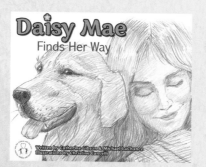

A portion of the proceeds from each book sold go to children causes.

To learn more about Cathy's stories please
visit her website at: **www.forchildrenwithlove.com**